E
Eve   Everett, Louise

        Bubble Gum In The Sky

A First-Start Easy Reader

This easy reader contains only 65 different words,
repeated often to help the young reader develop
word recognition and interest in reading.

Basic word list for *Bubble Gum in the Sky*

a	cried	hungry	she
again	day	I	smaller
all	down	left	south
and	ever	liked	sweet
asking	fat	little	that
at	feet	Lou	the
bee	flew	me	then
big	get	mouth	till
bird	got	night	to
blew	grew	north	touched
blow	ground	now	up
bubble	gum	opened	was
bubbles	happy	pecked	will
buzzed	he	popped	without
chew	help	right	word
cold	his	said	you
			yourself

Bubble Gum in the Sky

Written by Louise Everett

Illustrated by Paul Harvey

Troll Associates

Library of Congress Cataloging in Publication Data

Everett, Louise.
  Bubble gum in the sky.

    Summary: A rabbit with a fondness for bubble
gum blows a gigantic bubble which carries him
up into the sky.
    [1. Bubble gum—Fiction.   2. Rabbits—
Fiction]   I. Harvey, Paul, 1926-   , ill.
II. Title.
PZ7.E918Bu   1987   [E]   86-30859
ISBN 0-8167-0998-X (lib. bdg.)
ISBN 0-8167-0999-8 (pbk.)

Lou liked to chew.

He liked to chew gum.

He liked to chew bubble gum.

Lou blew bubbles.

He blew little bubbles.

He blew BIG bubbles.

Lou blew bubbles that popped!

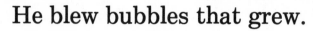
He blew bubbles that grew.

He blew and blew and blew.

The bubble grew and grew

and grew . . .

And Lou flew . . . up and up and up.

Lou flew to the left.

He flew to the right.

He flew all day.

And he flew all night.

Lou flew to the north.

He flew to the south.

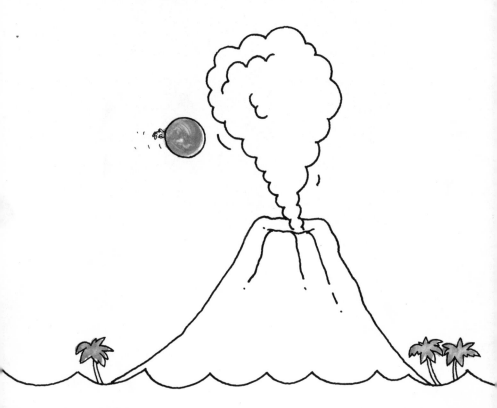

He was hungry and cold,

and he opened his mouth.

"HELP!"

"You got yourself up," buzzed a big
fat bee.

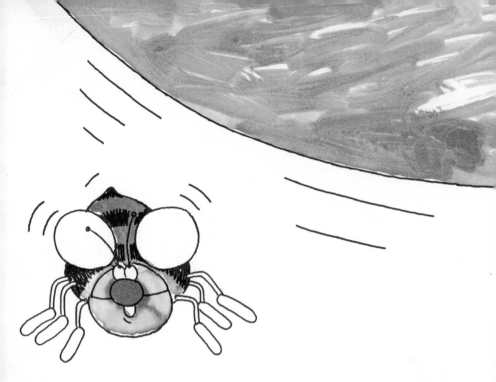

"Now get yourself down, without
asking me."

"HELP!" cried Lou
to a sweet little bird.

And she pecked at the bubble
without a word.

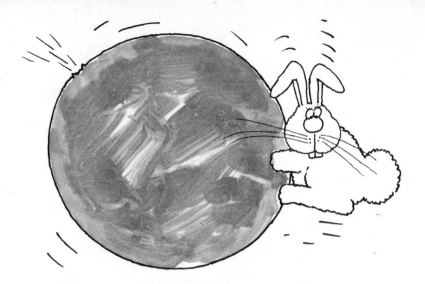

The bubble got smaller and smaller
and smaller.

And Lou flew down . . .

till his feet touched the ground.

Lou was happy, and then he said,
"Will I ever blow bubbles again?"